An **Andrex** Publication

PUPPY GOES TO THE SEASIDE

Written by
Gerald Durrell

Illustrated by Cliff Wright

y name is Puppy and I live with Nick and Susan, Mum, Dad and Grandad. They are my family.

One day Nick and Susan said, "Puppy, we're going to give you a bath."

They brought out the big white plastic bowl and filled it with water. I love having a bath and I splashed a lot. There was water everywhere and all over Nick and Susan.

As soon as I was out of the bath, they told me a secret.

"We are going to the seaside Puppy, and we're taking you with us."

I was very excited. Before Nick could dry me,
I ran into the house to see if all the family knew.

Only Grandad was there, reading the paper.
I rushed up to him and shook myself.

"So you've heard the news, Puppy," said Grandad.
"Now if I can dry my glasses, I'll be ready."

So he did know! I wondered if the sea was as wet
as when I had a bath. Did it taste of soap like my
bath water?

Nick came up and dried me.
He was excited too.

hen I went to make sure Mum and Dad were getting ready. "Oh Puppy! Please calm down," they said. "It's nearly time to go."

At last everything was ready and put into the car. Dad started the car but Mum shouted, "Stop!" She'd forgotten something.

Mum jumped out of the car, and came back with a beautiful red collar! It had a special medal hanging from it. My name was on one side and my address on the other side, just in case I got lost.

The seaweed was the brown kind with big bubbles in it. Nick and Susan squeezed the bubbles and they went pop like a cork! Then I bit them and we all made lots of popping noises.

"Listen, there's the ice-cream van," said Nick. They ran off up the beach but they forgot the sandwiches - and me!

Then a very large grey and white bird with a yellow beak landed near me.

"Is that my dinner in the bag?" he asked.

"Are you Seagull?" I said.

"Yes, and when I see people with paper bags like that, I know they have food for me."

"Well, help yourself. Nobody else wants them because they're squashed."

"I don't mind," said Seagull. "I think they're delicious. But I must go and get my wife to share them."

He flew off into the air with flaps of his great wings.

Under the water I could see a big creature like a huge spider, with great pincer-like claws in front.

"I was only trying to fly," I said.

"Ha!" bubbled Crab. "Whatever next! Puppies can't fly, everyone knows that."

"I didn't know," I said. "Do you live by yourself in this pool, Crab?"

"No, no," he bubbled. "Other crabs live with me and the sea snails of course, and sometimes little silvery fish come to visit."

Before he could grab me again, I scrambled out of the water, shook myself and ran off...

So, slowly and carefully I backed up the rocks, pulling him with me.

Just as we got to the top and safety, Nick and Susan came running up.

The poor terrier puppy sat panting for breath and I was panting too. Then it nuzzled up to me and said, "Thank you, Puppy," and scampered off.

"You brave puppy," said Susan patting me.
"You rescued him!"

Well, I didn't really. But when we arrived back
at the car, Mum got out the chocolate biscuits and
I felt like a hero. I rushed around barking.

As soon as we got home, I dashed into the garden
to find my friend Blackbird.

I told him all about our day, Seagull and Crab too,
but specially about my brave rescue.

"I really must try to go there," he squawked.

"You should," I said. "The sea is wonderful.
I had a great adventure."

And I trotted off to my cosy basket and tea.
Mum, Dad, Grandad, Nick and Susan all came
to say goodnight. "Sweet dreams," they said,
and I dreamed about my great big medal.